THE ADVENTURES OF SCAMP

'Oh, go away, you make me tired,' said the big dog. 'Pups like you always boast and think there is nobody like them in all the world. Go away or I'll snap your ears off!'

'I'll snap yours off first!' barked Scamp, in a temper, and he snapped so hard and so quickly at the big dog's ear that he managed to get a few hairs into his mouth.

The big dog turned on him at once. All the fur rose at the back of his neck and along his back. He stared at Scamp, and lifted his upper lip so that he showed all his great strong teeth. He looked terrible.

Enid Blyton Titles published by Red Fox
(incorporating Beaver Books):

The Magic Faraway Tree
The Folk of the Faraway Tree
Up the Faraway Tree
The Enchanted Wood
The Wishing Chair Again
Magic Faraway Tree Stories (3 in 1)
The Adventure of the Secret Necklace
The Adventure of the Strange Ruby
Four in a Family
The Four Cousins
Hollow Tree House
The Little Green Imp and Other Stories
Snowball the Pony
Buttercup Farm Family
The Caravan Family
The Pole Star Family
The Queen Elizabeth Family
The Adventurous Four
The Adventurous Four Again
The Children of Cherry Tree Farm
The Children of Willow Farm
House at the Corner
Josie, Click and Bun Stories (2 in 1)
Mr Twiddle Stories (2 in 1)
The Naughtiest Girl in the School
The Naughtiest Girl in School is a Monitor
The Six Bad Boys
Come to the Circus
Hurrah for the Circus
Mr Galliano's Circus
Circus Days Again
Runabouts's Holiday
Hedgerow Tales
More Hedgerow Tales
The Goblin Aeroplane and Other Stories
The Birthday Kitten and The Boy who wanted a Dog (2 in 1)
Holiday Stories

THE ADVENTURES OF SCAMP

Enid Blyton

Illustrated by Beryl Sanders

RED FOX

A Red Fox Book
Published by Random Century Children's Books
20 Vauxhall Bridge Road, London SW1V 2SA
A division of the Random Century Group

London Melbourne Sydney Auckland
Johannesburg and agencies throughout the world

First published by Newnes 1943
Red Fox edition 1992

© Darrell Waters Limited 1940

Enid Blyton's signature mark is a
Registered Trade Mark of Darrell Waters Limited.

Set in Plantin
Typeset by JH Graphics Ltd, Reading

Printed and bound in Great Britain by
Cox & Wyman Ltd, Reading

ISBN 0 09 987860 7

Contents

1 Scamp gets his name   7
2 Scamp gets into mischief   17
3 Scamp gets into trouble   29
4 Scamp grows up   43
5 Scamp does his best   52
6 Scamp is a policeman   64
7 A little quarrel   72
8 Scamp is a hero   79

CHAPTER 1

Scamp gets his name

When Scamp was born, he had no name at all, any more than you had. He lay in a dark kennel with his mother, Flossie, the wire-haired terrier. By him were three other puppies, squeaking as they wriggled about.

In the morning Mrs Hill came to look into the kennel, and she cried out for joy. 'Oh! Flossie's got four beautiful puppies! John, come and see!'

Her husband came up and looked into the kennel. He could just see the four little puppies lying beside their proud mother.

'My, they're beauties!' he said. 'Two are black and white, and two are brown and white. Which shall we give to Kenneth and Joan?'

'Oh, we'll wait and see,' said Mrs Hill. 'They had better choose for themselves.'

Soon the two children came racing up to see the new puppies too. Their mother and father had promised them one of them for their very own, and they were excited about it. Now that the puppies were really there, they could choose the one they wanted most.

Flossie let them look at her four puppies. 'They've all got their eyes closed!' said Kenneth.

'Well, puppies and kittens always do have their eyes shut at first,' said Joan. 'Aren't they sweet? I'll pick one up and cuddle it.'

But Flossie growled when Joan tried to pick up the nearest puppy, and the little girl put it down again in a hurry. 'All right, Flossie,' she said. 'I won't hurt it. I only just want to choose one for ourselves.'

'Let's wait till their eyes are open and they can run about,' said Kenneth. 'Then we'll choose the best!'

Every day the two children went to see Flossie and the puppies. They soon grew!

'I'm sure they are growing while I look at them!' said Joan. 'And, oh, look, Kenneth – this one has got its eyes just a little bit open! It will see tomorrow!'

It was seeing already, but not very clearly. By the next day his eyes were wide open, for Flossie had licked the eyelids of the puppy with her pink tongue, and he was able to look around.

He had been able to smell before – the

nice warm exciting smell of his mother and the other puppies. He had been able to taste too, and to hear the squeals of the others, the voices of the children, the growls of his mother. Now he could see – and that was very exciting indeed!

The other three had their eyes open wide the next day. Then they began to try and waddle round the kennel. They didn't know how to use their legs at first, and they kept falling over. The children laughed when they saw them.

'Flossie, do let us take your pups on to the lawn!' they begged. 'It will be good for them to waddle about there.'

Flossie didn't mind the children having the puppies now that they were growing well. So Kenneth and Joan took them one by one on to the lawn. But the sunlight was too strong for their newly opened eyes. So they put them into the shade, and then the pups were happy.

They tried to run here and there. They fell over and got up again. They ran into the tree trunks and bumped their noses. They smelt at a hurrying beetle and wondered what it was. They tried to climb on to the children's laps, and altogether were lovely to play with.

'Well, which are you going to have?' asked Mother, as she came to watch too.

'Oh, Mother, we don't know,' said Joan. 'They are all so sweet. I love this one with the black patch on his back, and this one too with the brown tail. And this little fellow is sweet with a black patch over one eye. The other one is rather small.'

'Yes, I wouldn't have her,' said Mother.

'She isn't so well-grown as the others. And don't have the one with the black patch on one side. His head is a little too big. Choose one of the others.'

Still the children didn't know which to choose. Kenneth wanted one and Joan wanted the other. And then they both discovered that the puppy with the black patch over one eye was the naughtiest of the lot!

'Let's have *him*, shall we?' said Joan. 'I'd rather like a naughty puppy – wouldn't you, Kenneth? He'd be more exciting than a good one. Look at him, the little monkey – he's pulling the head off that flower. You scamp! Come here! Oh, stop him, Kenneth, he's just going mad in that flower-bed!'

Kenneth ran to get the puppy. It tore away from him and disappeared into the wood-shed. It tried to get under the pile of firewood there – and by the time that Kenneth reached the shed, the wood was scattered all over the floor, and the puppy was angrily chewing up the piece that had hit him on the head!

'You really are a scamp!' said Kenneth,

picking up the puppy, which at once tried to chew his sleeve. 'Look at the mess you've made with that neatly stacked firewood. Now I shall have to tidy it all up. Joan! Take this pup, and keep him quiet. He's a real scamp.'

'Kenneth! Do let's choose this one and call him Scamp!' said Joan. 'I believe he'll be the nicest puppy of the lot. Let's have him.'

'All right,' said Kenneth, with a laugh, as he watched the puppy pulling at the buttons on Joan's dress. 'Look out – he'll have those buttons off!'

Mother came up just then. 'Children!' she said, 'two of the puppies are going away to new homes this afternoon. Have you chosen yours yet?'

'Yes, Mother!' said Joan, and she held up the puppy in her arms. 'This one! He's awfully naughty.'

'Well, for goodness' sake don't choose him then,' said Mother, in alarm. 'I don't want my best hat chewed up, and all the mats nibbled!'

'Oh, Mother, we'll see he doesn't do

anything *too* naughty!' said Joan, hugging him. 'But we do want him. He's really funny – and so loving. See how he licks me!'

'Yes, he's a dear little fellow,' said Mother, 'I should think he will grow into a fine rough-haired terrier very like his mother. I like that funny black patch over his eye too. It gives him such a cheeky look.'

The puppy looked up at her and barked in a funny little high bark.

'Oh, Mother! That's the very first time he's barked!' cried Kenneth, in surprise. 'He looks rather astonished at himself, doesn't he! I don't expect he knew he could bark!'

Everybody laughed. 'Yes, we really must keep him,' said Mother. 'He's going to be an interesting little creature, fearless and faithful. He's the cleverest of the batch too. What are you going to call him?'

'Well, there's only one name for him!' said' Kenneth. 'Scamp! Because he is a scamp, Mother.'

'All right. Scamp is a good name for a dog,' said Mother. 'Nice and short, and easy to call. Scamp! You'll soon know your name!'

Scamp almost seemed as if he knew it already. He rushed at Mother and tried to pull the laces out of her shoes. 'Don't!' she said, trying to take her feet away. 'Oh, you little mischief! Leave my feet alone!'

But as fast as she tried to take her feet away Scamp went after them, barking in his funny little high voice, his short tail wagging hard. The children shouted with laughter. In the end Kenneth had to pick him up to let Mother go back to the house in safety.

'I'm glad we've choosen you,' said Joan, tickling the puppy round the neck and under his hairy little chin. 'You're our dog now. Our very own. Did you know that?'

'And you're mine!' barked the puppy proudly. 'You belong to me! I'll look after you all my life long.'

CHAPTER 2

Scamp gets into mischief

Two of the puppies went away in a big box that afternoon to their new home. Scamp wandered about trying to find them. He had only a little sister-puppy left now, and she was the small one, and ran to shelter behind her mother if Scamp got too rough.

He liked to jump out at her and roll her over. Then he would nibble her ears and her tail, and make her squeal loudly. Flossie nipped him hard once when he was doing this, and gave him a real shock. After that he didn't tease the other puppy quite so much.

But when two disappeared to new homes he only had the little puppy left to play with, and Mother said that they must find a home for her because Scamp was so much bigger and stronger that he really was making her afraid.

So three days later the small puppy went too, and then only Scamp was left. The children were rather sad when the three puppies were gone.

'It was such fun when they were all playing around, Mother,' said Kenneth.

'A bit too much fun!' said Mother. 'Life is much more peaceful now we only have one left.'

'Well, I'm glad that one is Scamp,' said Joan. 'We are lucky to be able to keep one. Now we have a dog, a puppy, and a cat!'

Scamp knew the cat quite well. She was called Fluffy because she had a soft, fluffy coat that stood out all round her. Her eyes were as green as cucumbers, and her tail was long and wavy.

At first Scamp thought that Fluffy was pleased when she wagged her tail, but he soon found out that she wasn't!

He used to dart all around her, wuffing hard, and then her tail began to wag slowly from side to side, as she grew angry. Then,

when Scamp darted at her, she wagged her
tail more quickly, and began to hiss.

But the puppy, seeing her wagging tail,
quite thought she was pleased and friendly,
and pounced on it. Then Fluffy swung
round, spat at him, and hit him hard on the
nose with her paws. Once she put out her
claws and scratched him so that his nose
began to bleed.

Scamp was astonished. He ran crying to
his mother, and she licked his hurt nose.

'You are a silly puppy,' she said. 'You
must know that cats wag their tails when
they are angry, not when they want to be

friends. Whenever you see a cat wagging her tail, keep right away from her.'

'Why do we wag our tails when we are pleased?' asked Scamp, settling down beside his mother. He loved her nice warm smell.

'Well, when two dogs meet one another, they are not sure at first that the other will not fight,' said Flossie. 'They cannot smile at one another, as two-legged people do, because if a dog opens its mouth and shows its teeth, it means that it is ready to bite! So dogs use their tails as signals, you see. They wag them to tell the other dog that they want to be friends, not enemies.'

'And the other dog sees and wags his tail back!' said Scamp. 'It's a good idea, isn't it! How do cats show they are friendly?'

'You will hear them purr,' said his mother. 'Now, if I were you, I'd leave Fluffy alone. You haven't claws like sharp needles, as she has – and it's no good chasing her because she can climb trees and jump on walls, and you can't. So she will only laugh at you.'

All the same, Scamp often did chase Fluffy, and it was only when the cat turned on him, flew at him, and put ten of her sharp

claws into his head that he really thought it
would be best not to run after her any more!

Scamp loved nibbling and chewing
things. He liked to go into the nursery and
see what he could find there to nibble.
Sometimes he found a doll's shoe and
nibbled that. Then Joan would be very cross
with him and scold him.

'You bad dog! Look what you've done.
You've spoilt Angela's best shoe. I'm
ashamed of you.'

Then Scamp would put his tail down and
look up at Joan with such sad brown eyes
that she would forgive him at once. And
a minute later he would be shaking the life
out of Kenneth's new ball, biting big holes
in it, and growling at it as if it were a wicked
rat!

Once Scamp went into a visitor's
bedroom. He heard somebody coming, and
hid under the bed. The footsteps went by,
and he began to sniff around. There was a
round box under the bed. Scamp worried at
it until the lid came off. There was
something rather exciting in the box.

'It looks like the flowers in the garden!'

thought Scamp, as he looked at the hat inside, all trimmed with gay flowers. 'But it doesn't smell like flowers. I wonder what it is.'

He dragged the hat out on to the floor. He took it into the middle of the room and looked at it. One of the flowers shook a little and he put his paw on it. Then he began to nibble at the red roses on the hat. They didn't taste very nice. A bit of wire in one of them pricked his tongue. That made Scamp angry. He danced round the hat, barking loudly. 'What! You dare to scratch me with your claws, like Fluffy does! I'll chase you! Yes, I'll chase you. Run away and I'll come after you.'

But the hat didn't run away. It wasn't any fun at all. Scamp was cross. He pounced on the hat and the wire scratched him again. Then Scamp lost his temper and began to tear at the hat with his sharp puppy-teeth. He growled as he chewed the roses and the violets, and Auntie May, the visitor, heard him.

She came running upstairs and into her bedroom. When she saw her best Sunday

hat on the floor, and Scamp chewing it hard,
she gave an angry shout.

'Oh, you bad dog! Oh, you wicked dog!
You've spoilt my lovely new hat! Oh, my,
wait till I catch you!'

She caught up a bedroom slipper and
slapped Scamp so hard with it that he yelped
loudly and fled out of the room and down the
stairs.

Mrs Hill heard the noise and came to see

what the matter was. When she saw what the puppy had done she was very sorry. 'I'll give you a new hat,' she said to Aunt May. 'Don't be upset any more. That puppy really is getting into too much mischief.'

Mrs Hill marched downstairs and found Scamp hiding under the table. She dragged him out and gave him a hard spanking.

'It's time you learnt what to do and what not to do,' she said sternly. The children came running in when they heard poor Scamp howling.

'Oh, Mother, what has he done?' they cried. When they heard, they looked at Scamp with stern faces. Scamp crouched down and whimpered. He felt very sorry for himself indeed.

He crept up to Kenneth and tried to lick his hand. But the boy took his hand away. Scamp was terribly upset. He went to his basket and lay down there, his head over the edge, his ears down, and his tail quite still.

He felt as if he would never be happy again – never. Even kind-hearted Joan wouldn't speak to him.

After an hour or two he crept out of his

basket and went over to Mother. She put out a hand and patted him. He was overjoyed and began to bark at once. His tail went up, and he panted for joy.

'Now you are forgiven,' said Mother, 'but you must remember not to chew things up any more – only your own bones and balls, Scamp. Nothing else.'

So the next time that Scamp wanted to chew anything, he remembered his spanking and how unhappy he had been, and he ran off before he got his teeth into it. He was a good little fellow at learning his lessons!

When Scamp was a little older, the children bought him a collar. At first he couldn't bear it. He didn't like to feel it on his neck. He tried to wriggle it off. He put up his paw and pulled at the collar. But it wouldn't come off.

'What are you trying to do?' asked the dog next door, when he met him, and saw him trying to get his collar off by rubbing it along the fence.

'I hate this collar-thing on my neck!' said Scamp. 'I just hate it!'

'Well, don't you want to be properly dressed, then?' said the big dog. 'Haven't you noticed that all grown-up dogs wear collars? All men wear collars too, but little boys like Kenneth usually wear jerseys. If you've been given a collar it means that you're getting to be rather a grown-up dog. It's only puppies that don't wear collars.'

After that Scamp didn't mind his collar. He wanted to be grown-up. He felt even more gown-up than Kenneth, who still wore only jerseys. And he felt far more important than Fluffy, who wore no collar at all.

'You wait till you see what your collar's for!' said the big cat, swinging her tail. 'It's just to put a lead on when you go for a walk, so that you can't run off wherever you want to! You won't feel quite so pleased then!'

That was quite true. When Kenneth bought a lead and slipped it on to Scamp's collar, he felt cross. That horrid lead! Whenever he wanted to run ahead it dragged him back. Certainly he didn't like his collar any more.

But then Joan hung something on his collar that shone and tinkled. He wondered what it was. Flossie, his mother, told him.

'That's to say who you are, and where you live,' said Flossie. 'All dogs have to wear their name and address, you know.'

'Why?' asked Scamp, in surprise.

'Well, because their masters and mistresses love them, and don't want to lose them, of course!' said Flossie. 'If you should happen to be lost, anyone can look at the medal with your name and address on, and can bring you safely back home. Then Kenneth and Joan would be happy. Cats don't wear their names and addresses on collars. That must be because *we* are the important animals of the house, and not the cats.'

So Scamp was pleased with his collar again and showed his name and address to Fluffy.

'Pooh!' said Fluffy. 'Fancy having your name and address like that! Why, if *I* got lost, I'd know my way back without having to let people read my name and address, I can tell you! Dogs are poor creatures!'

'Woof!' said Scamp, in an angry voice. 'You're a horrid cat. I'm going to chase you.

And I'll nibble your tail *right* off this time! So look out!'

And Scamp really sounded so fierce that Fluffy thought she had better go. She ran off, her tail high up in the air, and Scamp pattered after her. Fluffy ran straight up a tree, and Scamp tried to follow. But he fell back to the ground at once and rolled over.

Fluffy sat up on a branch and laughed at him. 'You may be an important dog with your name and address on your collar!' she mewed, 'but I can climb a tree, and you can't!'

CHAPTER 3

Scamp gets into trouble

Scamp soon learnt to come whenever he was called, and to know the children's whistle at once. Wherever he was, he would come rushing to the children as soon as he heard them whistling to him.

But it was difficult to teach him not to chase anything that ran away! When Kenneth and Joan took him down to the farm lane, he saw hens wandering about all over the place. They scurried away, squawking when they saw Scamp coming, his nose to the ground!

'Ha! They're afraid of me! What fun!' wuffed Scamp to himself. 'I chase anything that runs away.'

And off he went after the hens. How they

scurried and flurried away! How they squawked and screeched! Scamp had a perfectly wonderful time.

'Scamp! Scamp! Stop it! Bad dog! Come here!' cried the children. But Scamp didn't hear a word. He had caught a hen by the leg, and was trying to get rid of a mouthful of feathers without letting go the hen.

'Oh! He's got a hen!' cried Kenneth. 'Goodness, we shall get into trouble if we don't stop him. *Scamp! Bad dog!* Come here at once.'

The wriggling hen made Scamp feel terribly excited. He still held on to it, enjoying its squawkings and clucks. The others ran away, terrified. Kenneth ran up to Scamp. He had the lead in his hand and he hit the excited dog once with it. It made Scamp jump. He let go the hen's leg at once and turned to look up at Kenneth.

'Woof!' he said. 'You hurt me! I'm sure you didn't mean to.'

'Oh yes, I did,' said Kenneth sternly. 'You were hurting that poor hen – so I had to hurt you to make you pay attention to what I was saying. Bad dog! Very bad dog! You will have to go on the lead all the way home!'

Scamp hated that. He put his tail down and went home very miserable. But all the way he kept thinking of the hens running away from him, and he longed to go down the lane again and chase them all once more! It was bad, he knew that. But perhaps if Kenneth didn't know, it wouldn't matter.

So he decided to slip off alone one morning and see if those exciting hens were still there. Off he went, his nose to the ground, smelling everything as he ran.

He soon came to the farm lane – and there, near the farmyard, were those red-brown hens wandering about loose again everywhere! What fun!

There were some tiny chicks too – little yellow and brown things, saying 'cheep-cheep-cheep!' They might be fun too, to chase, Scamp ran up to them.

Then something happened. A big fat hen ran at him, squawking at the top of her voice. How she squawked! It almost deafened Scamp. He stopped and looked at the hen. Then he made a little run at her, thinking she would turn tail and rush off like the others.

But the hen was the mother of the chicks, and she was very angry with Scamp for frightening her little ones. She was quite fearless. She didn't care how big a dog he was, or how many teeth he had – she was going to protect her little chicks!

So when Scamp ran at her, she ran at him. She put out her strong neck and pecked him hard on the nose. It made him yelp. Then she struck at him with one of her feet, and flapped round him with her big wings.

Scamp was most astonished. He got another peck that took some hair out of his ear, and he yelped. The other hens came to watch, clucking in delight.

Scamp ran back a few steps. The big hen followed, squawking loudly. She gave him a quick and spiteful peck again. 'I'll teach you to chase my chicks!' she cried. 'I'll teach you

to frighten them.' Peck – squawk – peck – squawk!

Scamp had had enough of it. He turned and fled down the farm lane, and the old hen scampered after him, screeching rude names. But she couldn't catch him up, of course. She soon went back to her chicks, and all day the other hens clucked together about the silly dog who had run away when the mother-hen had pecked him.

'That'll teach him a lesson,' they said. And

it did! Scamp never once chased a hen again. Kenneth was very pleased when he took him down the farm lane, to see the way he kept close to heel.

'I soon taught him not to chase hens,' he said to Joan. But it wasn't Kenneth who had taught him – it was the fat old hen!

Another thing Scamp had to learn was not to go into the fields where sheep are. Sheep are terrified of dogs, and soon bunch together and run off if any dog comes after them.

Two dogs were rascals at chasing the sheep. One was a big dog called Tinker, and the other was a small Scotty called Jock. Each day they slipped through the hedge into the field and made for the nearest group of sheep.

As soon as the sheep saw the dogs, they turned and ran. They frightened all the other sheep by their running, and it wasn't long before the whole flock was tearing about from side to side of the field, trying to get away from the barking dogs.

One day Scamp met Scotty, and the little dog spoke to him. 'You like a bit of fun, don't you? Well, come along with us, and you'll see some!'

'Good!' said Scamp, feeling grown-up and important. He scampered along with Scotty and Tinker, and they took him to the field where the sheep were feeding.

'Go through this hole in the hedge,' said Scotty. 'That's right. Now, you see those big grey creatures feeding over there? Well, just run after them and see how they rush away. It's such fun!'

Soon the three dogs were having a wonderful time. The sheep tore all over the place. Then suddenly a loud voice came through the air.

'I'll shoot you! You wicked dogs! I won't have dogs in my fields at lambing-time.'

'Wagging tails, it's the farmer!' barked Tinker, 'Come away, quick! He may have a gun.'

The farmer hadn't a gun that morning, or in his rage he might have shot at the dogs. As it was he managed to catch Scamp as he wriggled through the wrong hole in the hedge. He looked at his name and address.

'Oho! So you belong to the Hills, do you?'

Well, I'll just give them one warning about you – and then, you bad little dog, I'll shoot you next time you chase my sheep!'

He gave Scamp a blow that made him yell. He tore off down the lane at top speed. He felt ashamed of himself. He knew he shouldn't chase sheep. He knew he shouldn't chase hens. What would Kenneth and Joan say if they knew? But they wouldn't know, because they hadn't been there.

But they soon did know. A knock came at the door that very afternoon and outside was the farmer, looking very stern and grim.

'Good afternoon, Mam,' he said to Mrs Hill. 'I've come to give you a warning about that dog of yours. He was chasing my sheep this morning. Well, next time I see him doing that, I'll shoot him. So if you value your dog's life, you must either lock him up till the lambs are born, or you must keep him out of my fields.'

'Oh, Scamp!' said Kenneth, in dismay, when his mother told him what had happened. 'How could you be such a bad dog? You know you mustn't chase anything like that. Mother, what are we to do with him?'

'Keep him in the garden for a few days,' said Mother. 'Maybe he will forget about the sheep then. And if you always take him on a lead when you pass the sheep, he won't be able to chase them.'

Scamp was miserable. He hated being cooped up in the garden. It was such fun to wander round the country as he pleased. He felt certain he would never, never chase sheep again.

One afternoon Kenneth left the garden gate open. Scamp was out like a shot. Where should he go? He saw Scotty and Tinker on the other side of the road and he trotted over to them.

'Where are you going?' he asked.

'Down to the farm,' said Tinker, 'Coming?'

'Well, I'm not chasing sheep any more,' said Scamp. 'The farmer came to complain about me.'

'Well, you needn't chase sheep,' said Scotty. 'Just come for a walk and smell all the lovely farmyard smells, They've got some pigs down there, and we always think the pigsty smells wonderful.'

Then they passed near a field where the grey sheep were. Tinker poked his nose through the hedge. 'They look good to chase this afternoon,' he said. 'Is the farmer anywhere about?'

'I don't want to chase sheep,' said Scamp.

'Well, don't then, baby,' said Tinker, 'You're only a puppy, aren't you? We don't expect puppies to be as brave as we are!'

'I'm just as brave as any dog in the world!' cried Scamp, and he pushed his way into the field with the others. 'I'll soon show you! I'll chase more sheep than either of you!'

And he darted at three sheep nearby and yelped so loudly that they turned and fled at once. Scamp kept at their heels, enjoying the chase thoroughly.

Then suddenly there was the loud crack of a gun! *Bang!* Scamp nearly jumped out of his skin. The farmer must have come to the field! *Bang!* The gun spoke again, and Scamp turned and ran for the hedge as fast as he could. *Bang!* The gun went once more,

and this time Scamp felt somthing stinging him in half a dozen places.

'I'm shot, I'm shot!' he panted to Tinker and Scotty. 'I'm shot all over! Oh, what shall I do!'

But Tinker and Scotty weren't going to wait to look after a puppy-dog. They tore back home with their tails down, glad that they hadn't been hurt.

Scamp had many little pellets in his legs and chest from the gun. He felt tired and hurt. He began to limp. He was very sorry for himself.

'Why did I chase those sheep? I didn't really want to. I said I wouldn't. It was only because the others said I was a baby. I wish

I *had* been a baby now and not gone after the sheep. Then I wouldn't have been hurt.'

Kenneth and Joan were very upset when Scamp came limping in. Mother had to bathe his little wounds and get out the bits of shot. His fur was thick, so he hadn't really been hurt very much, but he felt as if he had.

He lay in his basket with his ears and tail down, looking very sorry for himself indeed. 'Cheer up, Scamp!' said Kenneth, patting him. 'You might have been shot dead instead of slightly hurt. But do let this be a lesson to you! Don't go chasing things any more!'

'I won't,' said Scamp. 'Except cats. All good dogs chase cats. But I'll *never, never* chase sheep again!'

And he never, never did!

CHAPTER 4

Scamp grows up

Scamp grew fast. He was a strong little dog, and very healthy. He grew well, and the children were proud of him.

'You're getting grown-up now, Scamp,' said Kenneth. 'You're a year old! Fancy that! It doesn't seem very long since you were a tiny puppy in the kennel, with eyes that were shut!'

Scamp had a deep bark now. He had lost his puppy-teeth, and had his grown-up set of strong white ones, that he bared whenever he met dogs he didn't like. Scamp was a fighter, and the children were always a little afraid that he might get hurt, for he sometimes fought dogs much bigger than himself.

'Scamp, you're such a good clever dog, and yet you won't learn that it's silly to fight!' said Kenneth. 'Why do you want to fight? There's no sense in it!'

Scamp didn't fight when he was with Kenneth or Joan. He knew they would put him on a lead if he began a fight, and he hated that. The free dogs always laughed at the dogs on a lead.

But he did fight when he was alone. He was quite a good-tempered dog really, but he simply couldn't bear it if any other dog wouldn't treat him as if he were grown-up.

One day he was very silly. He met a big dog he knew, and signalled to him with his tail to show that he was friendly. But the other dog was not in a good temper that morning. He hadn't had anything to eat, and he was hungry and cross.

So he didn't signal back to Scamp, but kept his tail quite straight and looked away.

'Why don't you greet me this morning?' said Scamp. 'Are you in a bad temper?'

'I don't always want to be seen talking to a pup like you!' said the big dog, walking off. Scamp galloped after him in a rage.

'I'm not a pup! I'm a year old! I've got my dog-teeth, not my puppy-teeth. And they're as strong as yours! I've fought heaps of dogs already.'

'Oh, go away, you make me tired,' said the big dog. 'Pups like you always boast and think there is nobody like them in the world. Go away or I'll snap one of your ears off!'

'I'll snap yours off first!' barked Scamp, in a temper, and he snapped so hard and so quickly at the big dog's ear that he managed to get a few hairs into his mouth.

The big dog turned on him at once. All the

fur rose at the back of his neck and along his back. He stared at Scamp, and lifted his upper lip so that he showed all his great strong teeth. He looked terrible.

But Scamp was not afraid, even when the big dog growled a deep growl right down in his throat. He stood quite still, and his hair, too, rose at the back of his neck. For a moment the two dogs stood there, growling fiercely – and then Scamp flung himself on the big dog, snapping hard with his teeth.

The dog tried to snap at Scamp, but the smaller dog had him by the neck and would not leave go. The big dog shook him hard and lifted him right off his legs. Then they both rolled over, growling and yelping.

And soon poor Scamp was yelping in pain because the big dog had got his teeth into him. People came running out to see what was the matter.

'Oh, that big dog is fighting the little one!' cried a woman. 'What shall we do? He'll kill him!'

A man went up to try and stop the dogs, but he was afraid of being bitten. The two angry animals worried one another, and loud barks and growls came from them. Then down the street came Kenneth and Joan!

'Oh, Kenneth! Look! Poor Scamp is one of those dogs!' cried Joan, tears coming into her eyes. 'We must save him. We really must.'

A man looked over a nearby wall. 'Hallo, hallo!' he said. 'What a fight! I'd better stop it before there's any damage done!'

'How can you stop it?' cried Kenneth. The man gave a grin and disappeared. The children looked over the wall. They saw that the man had been washing his car down with a hose. This hose he was bringing to the wall.

'A little of this will soon bring them to their senses!' he grinned. 'Look out!'

The hose was gushing water out strongly from the spout at the end. The man dragged the hose over the wall and directed the end at the two growling dogs. A great gush of icy-cold water fell on them. At first they took no notice, and then, as the man went on hosing them, they began to choke and splutter. The water went into their mouths and

ears, and they had to leave go of one another in order to breathe.

The stood there, growling, soaking wet, with the drops dripping from their coats. They both shook themselves, and thousands of shining drops flew all over the place. Kenneth and Joan were soaked.

'Come here, Scamp, come here!' they

shouted. And the owner of the big dog shouted too.

'Here, Rover, here!'

The dogs took no notice of their masters, but stared at one another, their tails held quite still. They growled again. The man with the hose soaked them once more, and with a yelp the big dog turned and fled down the street. He couldn't face that icy-cold water any more! His master went after him. Scamp was left by himself, shaking water from his coat again.

Kenneth and Joan went to him. 'Poor Scamp! Your ear is bleeding. You've got a lot of fur torn out of your neck. Come home quickly and we'll bathe you. Poor old Scamp!'

Kenneth turned to the man with the hose. 'Thank you for separating the dogs,' he said. 'I should never have thought of that.'

'You're welcome!' said the man, and took his hose back over the wall. The children walked slowly home with Scamp, who looked and felt very miserable.

Soon he was lying in his basket, bathed and comforted. Mother looked at him. 'I don't feel we ought to give you too much sympathy, Scamp,' she said. 'I've a feeling that you were just as likely to start that fight as the other dog. You must learn to leave big dogs alone!'

Scamp was soon all right again. In a few days' time he met the big dog again – but to his surprise the dog signalled to him with his tail at once! He wagged it hard.

Scamp wagged his back, feeling astonished. 'That was a good scrap, wasn't it?' said the big dog. 'I shan't call you puppy-dog any more. I see you're grown-up now. It was brave of you to pounce on me. I'm so much bigger than you are. If that man hadn't separated us I might have eaten you up. Let's be friends now, shall we?'

'Oh yes!' barked Scamp, feeling proud. 'How the other dogs would envy me if I were your friend!'

'Come and walk down the street with me,' said the big dog. 'I'll show you off to my own special friends.'

He did. The other older dogs were nice to Scamp, and he wagged his tail so many times that it really felt quite tired at the end!

'He's not a puppy-dog any more,' said the big dog. 'He's grown-up, just as we are. Now, Scamp, you don't need to fight us again, to show you aren't a baby. We know you aren't. So just be sensible and good-tempered. You may grow into a bad-tempered dog if you keep fighting – and then your master won't keep you.'

After that Scamp didn't fight again, but became friends with all the dogs in the street. They didn't call him puppy-dog any more, but accepted him as one of themselves, a grown-up dog with fine strong teeth, a deep and fearsome bark, and legs that went like the wind!

CHAPTER 5

Scamp does his best

Once Kenneth and Joan were ill. They had
to stay in bed, and Scamp couldn't understand this at all.

'What's the matter with the children?
Why don't they get up!' asked Scamp, when
Fluffy came by. 'Are they so tired and
sleepy?'

Fluffy looked at him out of her green eyes.

'They've got the measles,' she said.

Scamp didn't know what that was. He
stared at Fluffy. 'Well, I've heard of *weasles*,'
he said. 'They're what I sometimes chase in
the fields. Are the measles cousins of the
weasles? Why have the children got them?
Are they keeping them for pets?'

Fluffy didn't really know what the measles

were either. She just swung her tail a little and washed her left side.

'You'd better go and ask them,' she said. 'You're such an ignorant dog. You never seem to know anything.'

'I think I'll go upstairs and see what these measles are,' thought Scamp. 'If they are anything like weasels, I might chase them round the bedroom. That would be fun.'

So he trotted upstairs and into the children's room. Mother had put Kenneth's bed in the same room as Joan's, so that they might be company for one another. They shouted in delight when they saw Scamp.

'Scamp! Why haven't you been to see us before? We've got the measles and Mother won't let us get up!' they cried.

'Woof!' said Scamp, and his nose twitched as he tried to smell where the measles were. But he couldn't seem to smell anything unusual at all. It was strange.

He poked his nose under Joan's bed. No, there wasn't a measle there. He went under Kenneth's bed. There was no measle there either! Then where could they be?

Kenneth and Joan shouted with laughter. 'Mother! Mother! I believe Scamp is looking for our measles!' cried Kenneth. 'He's hunting everywhere for something. Come out, Scamp. My measles aren't under the bed.'

Scamp came out, puzzled. He soon gave up wondering where the measles were, and put his paws up on Kenneth's bed. Kenneth patted him.

'Are you being a good dog?' he said. 'Are you guarding the house well, and barking at bad strangers?'

'Woof,' said Scamp, his head on one side as he listened to what Kenneth said.

He always did bark at strangers he didn't
know and whose smell he didn't like. He
knew all the tradesmen now and didn't bark
at them – except the dustman. He always
barked at him, and he couldn't understand
why mother let the dustman take away the
dustbin each week. It seemed to Scamp that
the dustbin belonged to the family, and the
dustman had no right to come and take it.

So he barked loudly every time the man
lifted the big bin on his back – but as he
always brought it back again, Scamp didn't
bite him!

'And have you chewed anything you
shouldn't?' said Joan, from her bed. Scamp
went and put his paws up on the eiderdown
there and wagged his tail.

He hadn't chewed anything he shouldn't,
so he didn't put his tail or ears down as he
did when he felt guilty. He had chewed his
bone – and a bit of wood he had found in
the garden – and Fluffy's blanket. But that
was all. He felt that he had been a really good
dog.

Just then Mother came in, carrying a book
for each of the children.

'Little presents for ill people!' she said. 'That's the nice part of being ill, isn't it, children? People bring you things! Auntie May is coming up in a minute – and she has something for you too!'

Auntie May came up – and she brought a big bunch of black grapes. The children squealed for joy to see them.

'Oh, thank you, Auntie May! We *shall* enjoy them!'

Scamp sat and listened to all this. So the children were ill. That wasn't nice. But it *was* nice to have presents, of course. It made

them feel better. Scamp scratched his left
ear and thought hard.

'I love Kenneth and Joan, and I would like
to help them to feel better too,' he thought.
'I will bring them presents as well. That will
be lovely for them. I will bring them the best
presents I can think of!'

Scamp stayed with the children until their
dinnertime. They loved to hear his paws
pitter-pattering over the room, and to feel
him bump against the bed when he stood up
against it to look at them, his tail wagging as
if it were set on a spring.

Mother sent him down at dinner-time.
Then she gave the children their dinner, and
let them have some black grapes at the end.
She settled them down on their pillows and
told them to have a rest.

'Oh, but Mother, Daddy said he would
give us something nice after dinner,' said
Joan. 'Can't we wait till he comes?'

'No, he's busy now,' said Mother. 'You go
to sleep and I'll put whatever Daddy has got
for you on your beds. Then you can have it
when you wake up for tea. But go to sleep
now.'

So the children settled down and were soon fast asleep. Scamp went up to the bedroom, but they didn't say a word to him. So he pattered out again.

'I'll get them my presents,' he thought. He went into the garden and tried to remember where he had buried last week's bone. Oh, yes – under the lilac bush.

He began to scrape madly there, and then stopped to sniff. Yes – his bone was still there. He could smell it. He scraped hard again.

At last he had got the bone up. It still smelt very good. He gave it a little nibble to see if it tasted nice. Yes – the children would be sure to like that. It was his very best bone, most precious to him. He was so afraid that Fluffy or Flossie would get it that he always buried it after he had had a good nibble at it.

'Well, that's one present,' thought Scamp, and he scratched his left ear again. 'I believe I know where there are some kipper-heads. Those would do nicely for a present. I think I smelt them somewhere next door. The cat there didn't eat them.'

He squeezed through a hole in the privet hedge and went sniffing about the next door garden. Under the yew-hedge he came across two or three old kipper heads. The cat next door was very well fed and didn't always eat the kipper heads she was given twice a week.

'Ah! These are fine!' thought Scamp, taking them into his mouth. 'Wagging tails! They taste so nice that I do hope they won't slip down my throat by mistake!'

They didn't. He carried them to where he

had left his bone and then wondered if he should give the children anything else.

'I'll give Kenneth my ball, and Joan shall have the largest biscuit out of my dish,' he said to himself. 'That will please them. They are such nice children and so good to me that I'd like to give them anything I've got.'

He went to fetch his ball and the biscuit. Then one by one he took his presents to the nursery. First he took the big bone and pattered into the bedrom. The children were still asleep. Scamp put the bone gently on Kenneth's bed. Then he pattered out again and down the stairs.

He fetched the three kipper heads and put those on Joan's bed. Then he fetched the chewed ball for Kenneth and the big biscuit for Joan.

'It's a bit nibbled round the edges, but I daresay she won't mind that,' thought Scamp, as he put it on the eiderdown. Then he went downstairs again to tell Fluffy what he had done.

The children woke up about four o'clock. Kenneth stretched himself and then sniffed hard.

'What a funny smell!' he said out loud. Joan woke up and sniffed too.

'Gracious! There *is* a funny smell!' she said. 'It's like kippers or something.'

'Kippers! In the bedroom!' said Kenneth scornfully. 'All the same – you're right. It's exactly like kippers.'

'I wonder if Daddy has brought us anything whilst we've been asleep,' said Joan, sitting up. She looked on her eiderdown and gave a cry of surprise. 'Good gracious! Whatever's this that daddy has brought me?'

She looked at the three kipper-heads and the large biscuit. Kenneth sat up to – and saw the big dirty bone and the chewed ball. How surprised the two children were! At first they thought that Daddy had played a trick on them.

Then Kenneth gave a shout. 'Joan! It wasn't Daddy. It must have been dear, darling old Scamp! He saw other people bringing us presents because we were ill – and he thought he'd like to too!'

He's brought me three kipper heads and a nibbled biscuit!' said Joan laughing till the tears came into her eyes.

'And look at this awful old bone!' said Kenneth, holding it up for Joan to see. 'And he's given me his ball too – the one he loves so much. Joan, isn't he a generous, loving little dog?'

'He's the best dog in the world,' said Joan. 'Mother! Mother, are you there! Do come and look at the presents Scamp has brought us. Oh, Mother, it's so funny!'

Mother laughed when she came in, but

she wasn't very pleased to see the dirty bone and kipper heads on the eiderdowns. She took them off and sponged the places where they had been.

'Scamp! Scamp!' called Kenneth, when he heard the sound of pattering feet on the landing. 'Thank you, Scamp, for all the lovely presents you have brought us! We think they are the nicest we have ever had!'

'Do you really,' barked Scamp, his tail wagging fast. 'I'm so glad. They were the best I could think of. Enjoy the bone, won't you, and the kippers and the biscuit. And play with the ball as much as you like!'

Well, the bone, the kipper heads, and the biscuits disappeared, and Scamp felt certain that the children had eaten them. He didn't know that Mother had put them into the dustbin! But the ball didn't disappear – and when the chilren were better you should have seen the games they played with Scamp and his ball. He had the finest time in his life – but he deserved it for being such a generous little dog. Don't you think so?

CHAPTER 6

Scamp is a policeman

One night Scamp had an adventure. He was lying asleep in his basket when he woke up suddenly. His ears had heard a strange noise whilst he was asleep.

'Now what woke me up?' wondered Scamp. He looked at Fluffy, asleep in the basket next to his. 'Fluffy!' he said. 'Did you hear anything?'

'Only you snoring,' said Fluffy, curling herself up more tightly. 'Go to sleep and don't disturb me.'

So Scamp settled down again. But his ears stayed pricked up, and soon he heard a sound that made him sit up straight.

It seemed to come from outside, not inside. Could there be anyone outside? If so,

who was it? Nobody came at night. The tradesmen only came in the daytime and so did visitors. If anyone came at night they must be bad. They must want to steal something.

Scamp didn't bark. He got out of his basket and pattered across the floor. Fluffy woke up again.

'Have you *got* to run about all night?' she

said crossly. 'I do wish you wouldn't keep on disturbing me.'

Scamp took no notice. He was wondering how to get out into the garden and see what that noise was. The front door was shut. The back door was shut. But maybe a window was open at the bottom. He ran round the house to see.

No – not a single window was open at the bottom. Scamp ran up to the half-landing and looked at the window there. Ah – someone had left that open. He could jump out.

'But it's rather a long way to the ground,' thought Scamp, and he tried to think what was just below the window. 'Oh – it's all right, though. There's a bush below. I shall fall into that!'

He scrambled up on to the window ledge and then jumped into the darkness. He fell into the bush and lost his breath for a moment. Then he wriggled out of the bush and ran on to the grass. He stayed there, his ears up, listening.

At first he heard nothing. Then he heard a whispering sound some way off. Who could be whispering in the middle of the night?

He came to the hedge and squeezed through. Now he could hear the whispering much better. Somebody was at the back of the house. Two people. Why were they there?

'I've nearly got this window-catch undone,' he heard a voice whisper. 'We'll soon be in!'

'It must be robbers!' thought Scamp. 'Yes that must be it. Robbers! My mother has always told me to be on the look out for them at our house – and here are some next door. What shall I do? I'd better bark!'

But before he barked he ran up to the two men to smell them. They might perhaps be the people next door who had lost their key and were trying to get in at a window.

'Something touched me!' suddenly said the first man. 'I felt something touch my leg! Oooh, I don't like it.'

'Don't be silly,' whispered back the second man. 'It must have been a mouse running by.'

Then Scamp sniffed round *his* legs, and

the second man almost jumped out of his skin. 'Something touched *me* then!' he said, in a scared voice. 'I say – let's hurry up with this job and go. I'm getting jumpy.'

Then Scamp barked. Well, you should have heard him. He had a loud bark, but that night it sounded twice as loud! 'Wuff, wuff, wuff! WUFF, WUFF, WUFF!'

The men dropped their tools in a fright. 'We must run!' said one. 'Quick – that tiresome dog will wake up the whole street!'

It was a very dark night, and the men could not see. They tried to run, but one of them fell head-long over the barking dog. He fell to the ground and struck his head against the brick edge of the path. He lay still, for he had cut his head badly and had knocked himself out.

'Jim! Jim! What's up!' whispered the other man, wondering why his friend didn't get up. 'Come on. We shall be caught.'

He knelt down by Jim and tried to shake him. Then Scamp had his chance. He flew at the robber and got him by the collar. He held on for dear life, his teeth closed like a trap. He had meant to bite the man's

neck, but the robber had dodged just in time.

The robber was terrified. He did not dare to shake off the dog for fear he might fly at him again and get his teeth really into him. So he staggered about the garden in a terrible fright, trying to get over the wall at the bottom with the dog clinging to him.

But by this time the whole street was awake. Lights sprang up, and people with torches came into the gardens. They heard the tremendous growling going on in the garden next to the Hills', and they ran to see what was the matter.

'It's thieves!' cried Mr Hill, switching his torch on to the half-forced window. 'Look – here's one on the ground. He's hit his head against something and knocked himself out. The dog must have tripped him up.'

'And there's the other thief, trying to get over the wall!' cried somebody else, switching his torch on to the man and the dog.

'The dog's got him!' cried Mr Hill. 'It's Scamp! Good dog, Scamp! Hold him, hold him!'

Then a big policeman arrived, and the two men were soon taken in charge by him. The man who had been knocked out sat up and found himself surrounded by the people from the houses around.

The men were taken off. The people went back to their beds, talking excitedly. Kenneth and Joan, who had woken up, but

hadn't been allowed outside, welcomed
Scamp with shouts and pats.

'Oh, you good, brave, clever dog! You
caught those two robbers! Oh, Scamp we *are*
proud of you!

CHAPTER 7
A little quarrel

Joan wanted Kenneth to go for a walk with her. It was such a lovely afternoon.

'No, I want to do some gardening,' said Kenneth. 'My lettuces want thinning out, and I've got to cut all the dead roses off my rose trees. You go by yourself, Joan. But don't take Scamp. I do like him playing around me whilst I'm gardening.'

'Oh, but he's such good company when I'm out for a walk,' said Joan. 'He just loves a walk too. Don't be selfish, Kenneth.'

'I'm not!' said Kenneth. 'It's you that are selfish – wanting to go off for a walk when you could help me with the garden – and then wanting to take Scamp with you too, when you know how he loves being with me.'

'Well, he loves being with me too,' said Joan. 'He loves a walk much better than he loves gardening.'

Scamp came trotting up, his tail wagging. When he heard the children quarrelling, his tail went down! He didn't like that at all.

'Come here, Scamp,' said Kenneth, and Scamp went running to him to be patted.

'Good dog! I'm going to do some gardening. Coming to help me? I'll give you a biscuit if you work well!'

'Woof!' said Scamp joyfully. He loved being in the garden when Kenneth was working, because the boy talked to him all the time, and that was fun.

'Oh, Kenneth, you are mean!' said Joan, almost in tears. 'You know how I love Scamp going out with me for a walk. Well, I shan't ask him to come, because he just wouldn't know what to choose, and he'd be unhappy. I'll go by myself.'

The little girl walked off. She went down the garden path and let herself out of the gate at the bottom. It led into the lane, which was a nice place for a walk.

Scamp stared after her. So Joan was going for a walk. and she hadn't asked him to come. Kenneth was gardening, and *had* asked him to stay. But Joan was unhappy, and the dog longed to go after her to comfort her.

He looked at Kenneth, who was bending over the garden bed, whistling. Why didn't Kenneth go with Joan for a walk, then Scamp could go too, and everyone would be happy? The dog sat down and drooped his ears.

Kenneth wasn't very happy either, really. He knew it was mean of him not to let Scamp go with Joan – and Joan hadn't even tried to make Scamp go with her. That was rather nice her.

Kenneth went on working and whistling. He began to think about Joan. He wondered where she had gone – down the lane, across the field, over the little level-crossing, and along by the river. It would be nice there this afternoon.

'I hope Joan doesn't meet those rough boys we saw there the other day,' thought Kenneth suddenly. 'It's all right when Scamp and I are there, because they wouldn't dare to call names after her or chase her then – but she's alone today.'

He began to picture Joan being chased by the rough boys, and he felt more and more uncomfortable. 'I should have let her take Scamp. It was selfish of me. I didn't need Scamp – but she might. Why did I do that? It was really horrid of me. After all, I'm her brother, and I ought to see she's safe always. And she was very unselfish about it.'

Kenneth looked at Scamp. Scamp wagged his tail a little. 'I suppose you feel, too, that you should have gone with Joan?' said Kenneth. 'Well, I feel that now. I wish I'd let you go with her. If I knew which way she'd gone, I'd go after her. But I should probably go the wrong way and miss her.'

'Woof!' said Scamp eagerly. '*I* shouldn't miss her. I could smell her footsteps, you know.'

Kenneth guessed what Scamp was saying. He stood up and patted the eager little dog, who was now jumping about joyfully.

'Go and find Joan!' he said to him. 'Go and find her! Tell her I sent you, and I'm sorry I was mean. You go and find her, Scamp!'

Scamp barked loudly, licked Kenneth's hand and set off like a streak of lightning down the garden path. He pushed open the garden door with his nose and shot out in the sunny lane. Fluffy was on the wall there, just by the door, and she stared at him in surprise.

'What's up with you?' she asked. 'Can you smell the butcher boy coming, or something?'

'No,' said Scamp, his nose to the ground. 'I am going to find Joan.'

'Oh,' said Fluffy, 'well, she went down the lane. I saw her.'

'You needn't tell *me* that !' barked Scamp. 'My nose has already told me! I can smell her footsteps – here they go – down this

side of the lane – and into the ditch to pick a flower – and over to the other side to see something else – and then down the middle of the lane. Here I go! I'll soon find Joan!'

CHAPTER 8

Scamp is a hero

Joan wasn't enjoying her walk very much. She felt cross with Kenneth, and she missed Scamp. It was such fun when he came for walks – he always danced round them, ran after sticks they threw, rolled over and over in the grass, and altogether went quite mad. It was lonely without him.

The river was lovely that afternoon. It flowed along, smooth and blue and glittering.

The little girl ran along by the water. She suddenly saw a moorhen swimming along near the bank, its little black head bobbing to and fro as if it went by clockwork. She laughed. 'You're sweet!' she said. 'Have you any babies? I wish I could see them. Moorhen chicks are lovely!'

The moorhen had some chicks. They were swimming after her in a long line, very small indeed. When the moorhen saw Joan she was frightened. She called to her chicks at once.

'Look out! That girl might be an enemy and throw stones. Our old nest is quite near here. Follow me and we will hide in it till she is gone.'

She swam to where the old nest, made of flattened rushes, lay hidden in a tiny cove nearby. The chicks scrambled up into it, and squatted down, quite quiet.

Joan wondered where they had gone. She went to see. She caught sight of the nest, and exclaimed in delight.

'Oh! You're all in your old nest! Oh, I really must get nearer and see you!'

She put a foot carefully on to a clump of rushes. Then her left foot went on to another clump of rushes. The little girl bend over to see the moorhen's nest and chicks.

Her foot suddenly slipped. She flung out her hands to try and get her balance, but she

couldn't, for the rushes were so slippery to tread on. She fell headlong into the water with such a splash that all the chicks were terrified and slipped out of their nest to hide under the water.

Joan struck out with her hands to try and get to the bank. She couldn't swim, but she thought she could soon get to the bank. The water was very deep there. She pulled hard at some rushes, but instead of helping her, they gave way, and she fell back into deeper water.

Then the current of the river caught her and began to move her away from the bank. She screamed. 'Help! Help! Oh, help me, someone! I'm in the water!'

And where was Scamp He had just gone over the little level-crossing, and was running to the riverside. He stood there and looked. There was no sign of Joan anywhere. She must have gone a very long way!

The dog put his nose to the ground and went along by the water, sniffing where the little girl had walked. Then suddenly a faint, far-off sound came to his ears. Why, it was Joan's voice. She must be in trouble! But where could she be? There wasn't a sign of her anywhere.

Scamp looked into the water – and there, swung out to the middle of the river by the strong current, was poor Joan still struggling hard.

'I'm coming!' barked Scamp loudly. And into the water he leapt at once. He swam strongly towards the little girl, his nose just

above the surface. He could not swim very
fast, but he did the best he could.

His heart was beating fast, and he was
panting when he reached the little girl. He
caught hold of her dress, and turned himself
round towards the bank. Somehow he must
get her there before she sank under the
water and disappeared!

It was hard work, for Joan was heavy and
her clothes were full of water. But the dog

would not give up. He worked his legs steadily, though he felt as if he really could not possibly swim even halfway to the bank with such a heavy load to drag. But it was Joan – the little girl he loved! He had to save her, even if his beating heart burst itself.

When they got near the bank Joan managed to clutch some strong tufts of rushes and pulled herself in. She lay on the sloping bank wet and frightened – but safe! Scamp shook himself, and then went to lick Joan. He was frightened too, and worried – but so glad that he had been able to save Joan when she was in danger. What a good thing Kenneth had let him go after her!

When Joan felt better, she stood up rather unsteadily, and began to walk slowly home. Scamp ran beside her. They met no one, and at last Joan went through the garden door and into the back garden of her home. Kenneth was still there gardening.

Joan sank down on the grass beside him and told him in a faint voice all that had happened. 'And if it hadn't been for dear old darling Scamp, I'd have been drowned,' she said. 'I'm sure I would. Oh, Kenneth, he was wonderful. He's a real hero! Dear old Scamp!'

Kenneth put his arms round Joan and lifted her up. 'It's all my fault!' he said. 'I should have come with you. Come indoors. You're shivering. You must change your clothes. Poor Joan.'

Joan was soon out of her wet clothes and into a warm bed. Mother fussed over her, and Joan began to feel she had had quite an adventure. When Daddy came home he had to hear all about it too, and he looked rather grave.

'You mustn't walk alone by the river again,' he told Joan. 'You must always take Scamp. Good dog! What should we do without you? You're a hero, Scamp! Did you know that? Yes – a real hero!'

Scamp didn't know what a hero was, but he thought it must be something nice as Mr Hill said it in such a proud voice. He wagged his tail hard, and ran off to find Fluffy.

'Hallo,' he said. 'Did you know I was a hero? The master just said I was.'

'Well, he's made a mistake,' said Fluffy,

washing her face. 'You're no hero! You're just a tiresome little dog with much too loud a bark!'

And that was all that Scamp got out of Fluffy! But the others made up for it – they gave him a fine new rubber ball, and emptied a tin of his favourite sardines into his dish, and bought him the biggest and juiciest bone he had ever had.

'You're better than a hero!' said Joan,

hugging him. 'Scamp, you're the dearest and the best dog that ever lived. How do you like that?'

Well – Scamp liked it very much indeed. I think Joan was right, don't you!

Enter the magical world of Dr Dolittle

Dr Dolittle is one of the great book characters – everyone knows the kindly doctor who can talk to the animals. With his household of animals – Too-Too the owl, Dab-Dab the duck, Gub-gub the pig and Jip the dog – and Tommy Stubbins, his assistant, he finds himself in and out of trouble, of money and of England in a series of adventures. These editions have been sensitively edited with the approval of Christopher Lofting, the author's son.

THE STORY OF DOCTOR DOLITTLE
ISBN 0 09 985470 8   £3.99

THE VOYAGES OF DOCTOR DOLITTLE
ISBN 0 09 985470 8   £4.99

DR DOLITTLE'S POST OFFICE
ISBN 0 09 988040 7   £4.99

DR DOLITTLE'S CIRCUS
ISBN 0 09 985440 6   £4.99

DR DOLITTLE'S ZOO
ISBN 0 09 988030 X   £4.99

DR DOLITTLE'S GARDEN
ISBN 0 09 988050 4   £4.99

DR DOLITTLE IN THE MOON
ISBN 0 09 988060 1   £4.99

DR DOLITTLE'S CARAVAN
ISBN 0 09 985450 3   £4.99

DR DOLITTLE AND THE GREEN CANARY
ISBN 0 09 988090 3   £4.99

Other great reads ✤ *from* **Red Fox**

Animal stories from Enid Blyton

If you like reading stories about animals, you'll love Enid Blyton's animal books.

THE BIRTHDAY KITTEN

Terry and Tessie want a pet for their birthday – but when the big day comes, they're disappointed.

ISBN 0 09 924100 5   £1.99

THE BIRTHDAY KITTEN and
THE BOY WHO WANTED A DOG

A great value two-books-in-one containing two stories about children and their lovable pets.

ISBN 0 09 977930 7   £2.50

HEDGEROW TALES

Go on a journey through the woodlands and fields and meet the fascinating animals who live there.

ISBN 0 09 980880 3   £2.50

MORE HEDGEROW TALES

A second set of animal stories packed with accurate details.

ISBN 0 09 980880 3   £2.50

Other great reads from **Red Fox**

All the fun of the fair with Enid Blyton's circus stories

Roll up! Roll up! Discover Enid Blyton's exciting circus stories for yourself. They're full of adventure and thrills, with a colourful cast of funny and unusual characters and lovable animals. Join the children who live in the circus and enjoy all the fun of the fair for yourself.

MR GALLIANO'S CIRCUS

Jimmy loves the circus – how can he bear it to leave town? Is there *any* hope he might go with it?

ISBN 0 09 954170 X £1.75

CIRCUS DAYS AGAIN

A new ringleader arrives at Mr Galliano's circus – and, oh dear! No one can *bear* him . . .

ISBN 0 09 954180 7 £1.75

COME TO THE CIRCUS

Fenella is terrified of animals. Imagine her horror when she discovers she is going to live in Mr Carl Crack's circus!

ISBN 0 09 937590 7 £1.75

THREE BOYS AND A CIRCUS

Orphan Dick is thrilled to find a job at the circus – but he has an enemy who wants him to leave.

ISBN 0 09 987870 4 £2.99

Other great reads ✦ *from* **Red Fox**

Magical books from Enid Blyton

Enter the world of fairyland with the magical stories of Enid Blyton – and enjoy tales of goblins, pixies, fairies and all sorts of strange and wonderful things.

UP THE FARAWAY TREE

If you climb to the top of the Faraway Tree, you can reach all sorts of wonderful places . . .

ISBN 0 09 942720 6   £2.50

THE GOBLIN AEROPLANE AND OTHER STORIES

Jill and Robert are working outside when they are whisked away on a strange adventure . . .

ISBN 0 09 973590 3   £2.50

HOLIDAY STORIES

A lovely collection of stories with some magical characters.

ISBN 0 09 987850 X   £1.99

THE LITTLE GREEN IMP AND OTHER STORIES

An enchanting collection of stories about some very special people – including the mischievous green imp.

ISBN 0 09 938940 1   £1.50

RUN-ABOUT'S HOLIDAY

Run-About is Robin and Betty's magical friend – and life is never dull when he's around!

ISBN 0 09 926040 9   £1.50

Adventure Stories from Enid Blyton

THE ADVENTUROUS FOUR

A trip in a Scottish fishing boat turns into the adventure of a lifetime for Mary and Jill, their brother Tom and their friend Andy, when they are wrecked off a deserted island and stumble across an amazing secret. A thrilling adventure for readers from eight to twelve.

ISBN 0 09 947700 9   £2.50

THE ADVENTUROUS FOUR AGAIN

'I don't expect we'll have any adventures *this* time,' says Tom, as he and sisters Mary and Jill arrive for another holiday. But Tom couldn't be more mistaken, for when the children sail along the coast to explore the Cliff of Birds with Andy the fisher boy, they discover much more than they bargained for . . .

ISBN 0 09 947710 6   £2.50

COME TO THE CIRCUS

When Fenella's Aunt Jane decides to get married and live in Canada, Fenella is rather upset. And when she finds out that she is to be packed off to live with her aunt and uncle at Mr Crack's circus, she is horrified. How will she ever feel at home there when she is so scared of animals?

ISBN 0 09 937590 7   £1.99

Other great reads *from* **Red Fox**

THE SNIFF STORIES   Ian Whybrow

Things just keep happening to Ben Moore. It's dead hard avoiding disaster when you've got to keep your street cred with your mates *and* cope with a family of oddballs at the same time. There's his appalling 2½ year old sister, his scatty parents who are into healthy eating and animal rights and, worse than all of these, there's Sniff! If only Ben could just get on with his scientific experiments and his attempt at a world beating *Swampbeast* score . . . but there's no chance of that while chaos is just around the corner.

ISBN 0 09 975040 6   £2.99

J.B. SUPERSLEUTH   Joan Davenport

James Bond is a small thirteen-year-old with spots and spectacles. But with a name like that, how can he help being a supersleuth?

It all started when James and 'Polly' (Paul) Perkins spotted a teacher's stolen car. After that, more and more mysteries needed solving. With the case of the Arabian prince, the Murdered Model, the Bonfire Night Murder and the Lost Umbrella, JB's reputation at Moorside Comprehensive soars.

But some of the cases aren't quite what they seem . . .

ISBN 0 09 971780 8   £2.99

Other great reads from **Red Fox**

Discover the exciting and hilarious books of Hazel Townson!

THE MOVING STATUE

One windy day in the middle of his paper round, Jason Riddle is blown against the town's war memorial statue.

But the statue moves its foot! Can this be true?

ISBN 0 09 973370 6   £1.99

ONE GREEN BOTTLE

Tim Evans has invented a fantasic new board game called REDUNDO. But after he leaves it at his local toy shop it disappears! Could Mr Snyder, the wily toy shop owner have stolen the game to develop it for himself? Tim and his friend Doggo decide to take drastic action and with the help of a mysterious green bottle, plan a Reign of Terror.

ISBN 0 09 935490 X   £2.25

THE SPECKLED PANIC

When Kip buys Venger's Speckled Truthpaste instead of toothpaste, funny things start happening. But they get out of control when the headmaster eats some by mistake. What terrible truths will he tell the parents on speech day?

ISBN 0 09 956810 1   £2.25

THE CHOKING PERIL

In this sequel to *The Speckled Panic*, Herbie, Kip and Arthur Venger the inventor attempt to reform Grumpton's litterbugs.

ISBN 0 09 950530 4   £2.25

Other great reads ✎ *from* **Red Fox**

School stories from Enid Blyton

THE NAUGHTIEST GIRL IN THE SCHOOL

'Mummy, if you send me away to school, I shall be so naughty there, they'll have to send me back home again,' said Elizabeth. And when her parents won't be budged, Elizabeth sets out to do just that—she stirs up trouble all around her and gets the name of the bold bad schoolgirl. She's sure she's longing to go home—but to her surprise there are some things she hadn't reckoned with. Like making friends . . .

ISBN 0 09 945500 5   £2.99

THE NAUGHTIEST GIRL IS A MONITOR

'Oh dear, I wish I wasn't a monitor! I wish I could go to a monitor for help! I can't even think what I ought to do!'

When Elizabeth Allen is chosen to be a monitor in her third term at Whyteleafe School, she tries to do her best. But somehow things go wrong and soon she is in just as much trouble as she was in her first term, when she was the naughtiest girl in the school!

ISBN 0 09 945490 4   £2.99

THE ENID BLYTON NEWSLETTER

Would you like to receive The Enid Blyton Newsletter? It has lots of news about Enid Blyton books, videos, plays, etc. There are also puzzles and a page for your letters. It is published three times a year and is free for children who live in the United Kingdom and Ireland.

If you would like to receive it for a year, please write to: The Enid Blyton Newsletter, PO Box No. 357, London WC2E 9HQ, sending your name and address. (UK and Ireland only).